For Riker
and all the animals
who bring us joy

Riker's Taxi Trouble © 2019 by Tracy Sides

ISBN: 978-1-64343-953-2
Library of Congress Catalog Number: 2019905758
Printed in Canada
First printing 2019
23 22 21 20 19   5 4 3 2 1

Edited by Laurie Buss Herrmann
Illustrated by Kevin Cannon
Cover and interior design by Kevin Cannon

BEAVER'S POND
PRESS

Beaver's Pond Press, Inc.
7108 Ohms Lane
Edina, MN 55439-2129
(952) 829-8818
www.BeaversPondPress.com

MIX
Paper from
responsible sources
FSC® C016245
FSC
www.fsc.org

To order, visit www.ItascaBooks.com or call (800) 901-3480, ext. 118
You may contact the author by e-mail at books@tracysides.com
or visit her website at tracysides.com.

RIKER'S Taxi Trouble

Tracy Sides

illustrated by
Kevin Cannon

It was a bright and beautiful morning,
a day like any other in Oak Grove.

But it didn't
stay that way
for long.

"Good morning,
Mr. Mouse," I said.
"What brings you to town?"

"I went to the dentist," he said.

"But now I need to get back to the field, and Riker is late picking me up."

Mr. Mouse's complaint reminded
me that my dog, Riker, had just
started a taxi business.

"Hmm," I thought. "Being late
is not good customer service."

All of a sudden, something yellow and fast squealed around the corner.

SQUEAL!!

It was Riker!

His taxi screeched to a halt,
the back door flew open, and
Mr. Mouse scampered inside.

Then, with a wave of his
paw, Riker sped off.

eeeeeeeeeeeeEEECH!!!

I took a walk to the woods to get my mind off Riker's taxi trouble.

What a surprise to see a family of dragonflies near the old oak tree.

"Hello, dragonflies,"
I said. "What brings
you to the forest? I usually
see you in the prairie or near the pond."

"Exactly!" said Mrs. Dragonfly. "That dog of yours runs a terrible taxi business.
He was supposed to drop us off at the pond, but instead, he brought us here!"

"I'm sorry, Mrs. Dragonfly," I sighed. "I don't know what's gotten into him."

Riker's taxi trouble was getting worse.

Mr. Mouse was picked up late. The dragonflies were taken to the wrong place.

"I better talk to Riker about his awful customer service," I thought as I headed for home.

At the crosswalk, a bushy tail brushed my elbow and I realized I was surrounded by a scurry of squirrels and chipmunks. The "Nuts of the Midwest" conference was apparently underway.

I turned to say hello
to Professor Squirrel,
but she was preoccupied.

"Oh dear!" she said.
"Mr. Squirrel and I are
supposed to present our
acorn research, but he
isn't here yet!"

Then the "walk" sign lit up, and
clusters of nut conference attendees
hustled across the street, carrying
Professor Squirrel away with them.

Suddenly, police sirens and
Mr. Squirrel's screams filled the air.

Everybody froze.

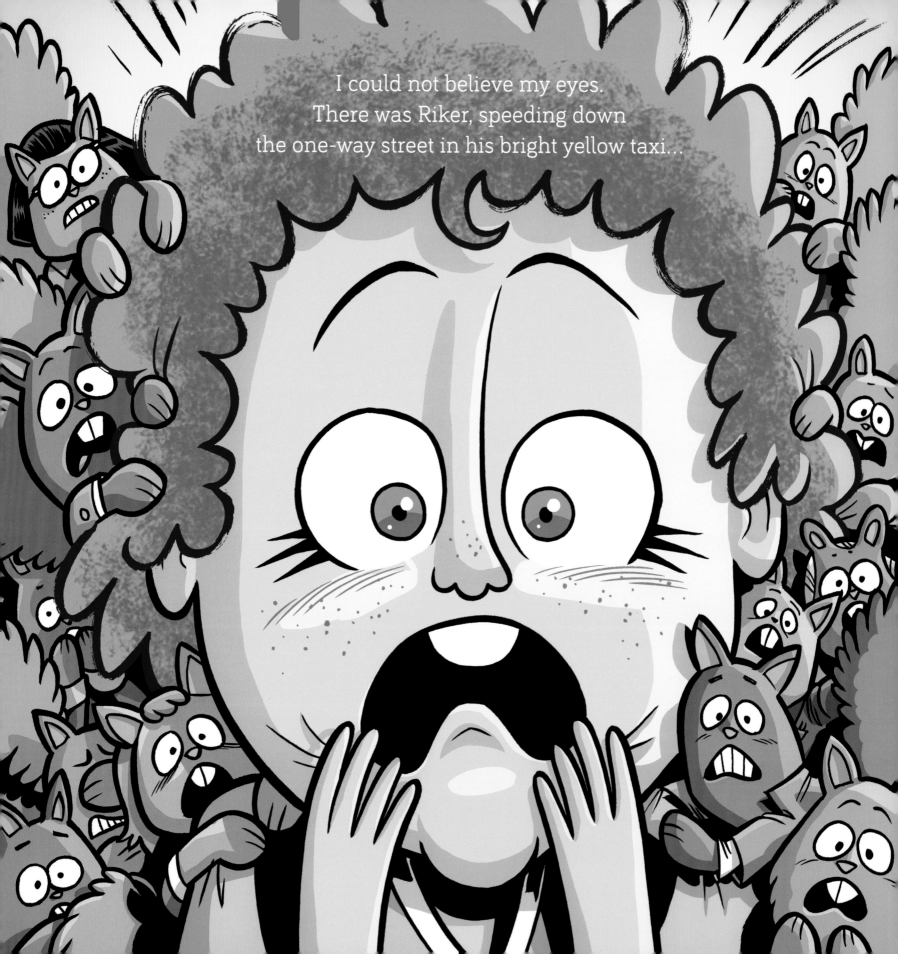

I could not believe my eyes.
There was Riker, speeding down
the one-way street in his bright yellow taxi...

The police were chasing Riker!

Poor Mr. Squirrel
was still screaming!

And I yelled, "Riker!
Riker! Pull over!
PULL OVER!"

Finally, he did.

Riker hopped out
of his taxi, pleased
with his adventures.

The police officer
was *not* pleased.

"No more shenanigans,
you pesky poodle!" he barked
as he leapt toward Riker.

But Riker just lay down
and rolled on his back.

So the police officer
flew right over him.

"Riker, you reckless rascal,"
I said, ready to scold him for all the taxi
trouble he'd caused—when he looked up
at me, wagging his tail, and asked,
"Is it belly rub time yet?"

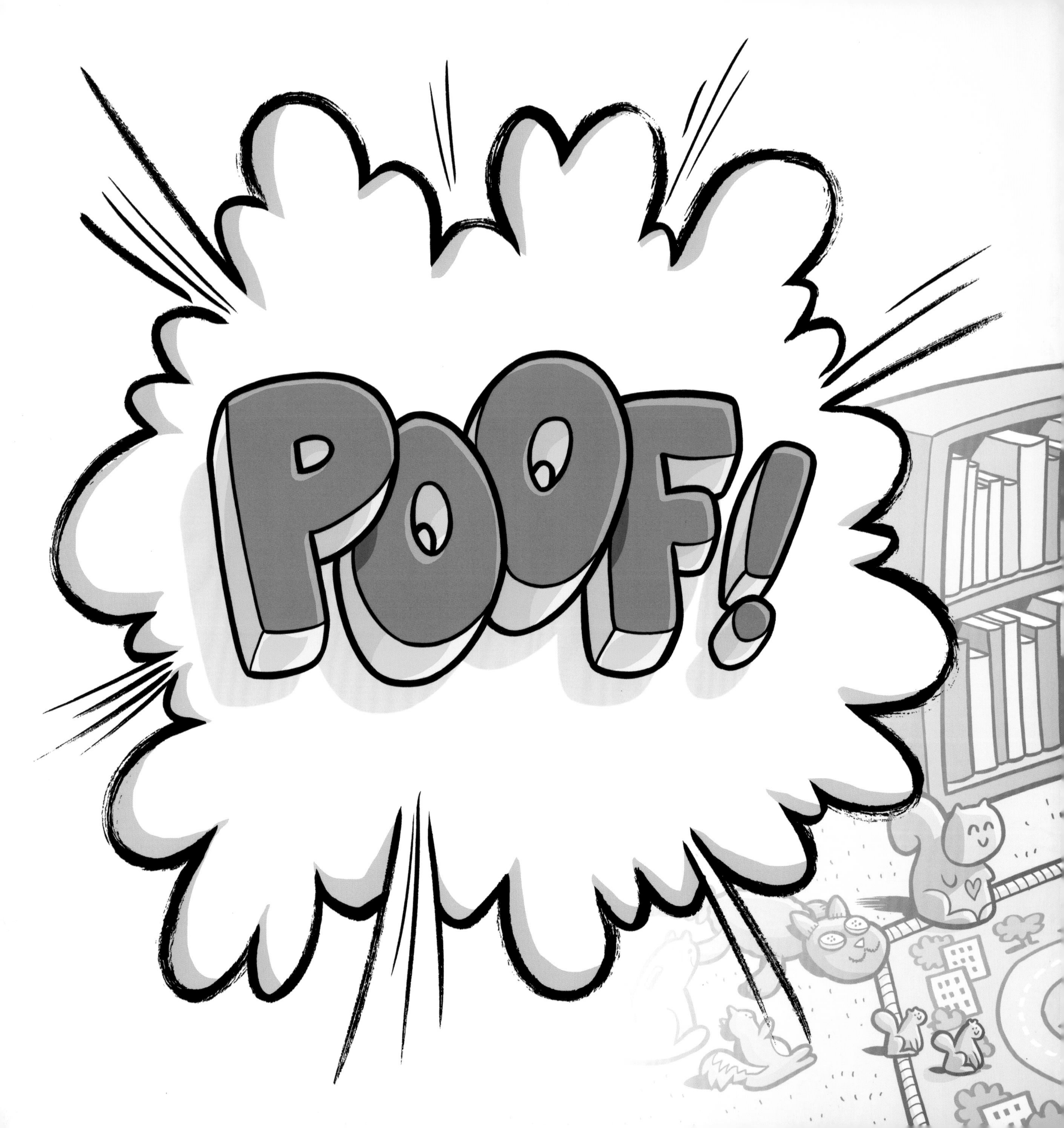
POOF!

I laughed and laughed.

"Yes, Riker," I said. "You're a terrible taxi driver. But I will always love you!"